P9-CRD-911

STAR WARS ADVENTURES

GHOSTS OF VADER'S CASTLE

Fountaindale Public Library District
300 W. Briarcliff Rd.
Bolingbrook, IL 60440

Facebook: **facebook.com/idwpublishing**
Twitter: **@idwpublishing**
YouTube: **youtube.com/idwpublishing**
Instagram: **instagram.com/idwpublishing**

COVER ARTIST
FRANCESCO FRANCAVILLA

LETTERER & PRODUCTION ASSISTANCE
SHAWN LEE

SERIES ASSISTANT EDITOR
RILEY FARMER

SERIES EDITOR
HEATHER ANTOS

COLLECTION EDITORS
ALONZO SIMON
& ZAC BOONE

ISBN: 978-1-68405-906-5 25 24 23 22 1 2 3 4

STAR WARS ADVENTURES: GHOSTS OF VADER'S CASTLE. JANUARY 2022. FIRST PRINTING. © 2022 Lucasfilm Ltd. ® or ™ where indicated. All Rights Reserved. The IDW Logo is registered in the U.S. Patent and Trademark Office. IDW Publishing, a division of Idea and Design Works, LLC. Editorial offices: 2765 Truxtun Road, San Diego, CA 92106. Any similarities to persons living or dead are purely coincidental. With the exception of artwork used for review purposes, none of the contents of this publication may be reprinted without permission of Idea and Design Works, LLC. IDW Publishing does not read or accept unsolicited submissions of ideas, stories, or artwork. Printed in Canada.

Originally published as STAR WARS ADVENTURES: GHOSTS OF VADER'S CASTLE issues #1–5.

Nachie Marsham, Publisher | Blake Kobashigawa, VP of Sales
Tara McCrillis, VP Publishing Operations | John Barber, Editor-in-Chief
Mark Doyle, Editorial Director, Originals | Erika Turner, Executive Editor
Scott Dunbier, Director, Special Projects | Lauren LePera, Managing Editor
Joe Hughes, Director, Talent Relations | Anna Morrow, Sr. Marketing Director
Alexandra Hargett, Book & Mass Market Sales Director | Keith Davidsen, Director, Marketing & PR | Topher Alford, Sr Digital Marketing Manager
Shauna Monteforte, Sr. Director of Manufacturing Operations | Jamie Miller, Sr. Operations Manager | Nathan Widick, Sr. Art Director, Head of Design
Neil Uyetake, Sr. Art Director, Design & Production | Shawn Lee, Art Director, Design & Production | Jack Rivera, Art Director, Marketing

Ted Adams and Robbie Robbins, IDW Founders

Lucasfilm Credits:
Robert Simpson, Senior Editor
Michael Siglain, Creative Director
Troy Alders, Art Director
Pablo Hidalgo, Matt Martin, and Emily Shkoukani, Story Group
Phil Szostak, Art Department

Written by Cavan Scott

Dawn of the Droids

Art by Francesco Francavilla [1-4, 19-20]

& Megan Levens [5-18]

with colors by Francesco Francavilla [1-4, 19-20]

& Charlie Kirchoff [5-18]

Attack of the 50-Foot Wookiee

Art and Colors by Francesco Francavilla [1–4, 19–20]

& Derek Charm [5–18]

Danger on Dagobah

Art and Colors by Francesco Francavilla [1–3, 19–20]

& Robert Hack [4–18]

Beware... The Chosen One

Art and Colors by Chris Fenoglio [1–14]

& Francesco Francavilla [15-20]

Vader Has Risen From The Grave

Art and Colors by Francesco Francavilla

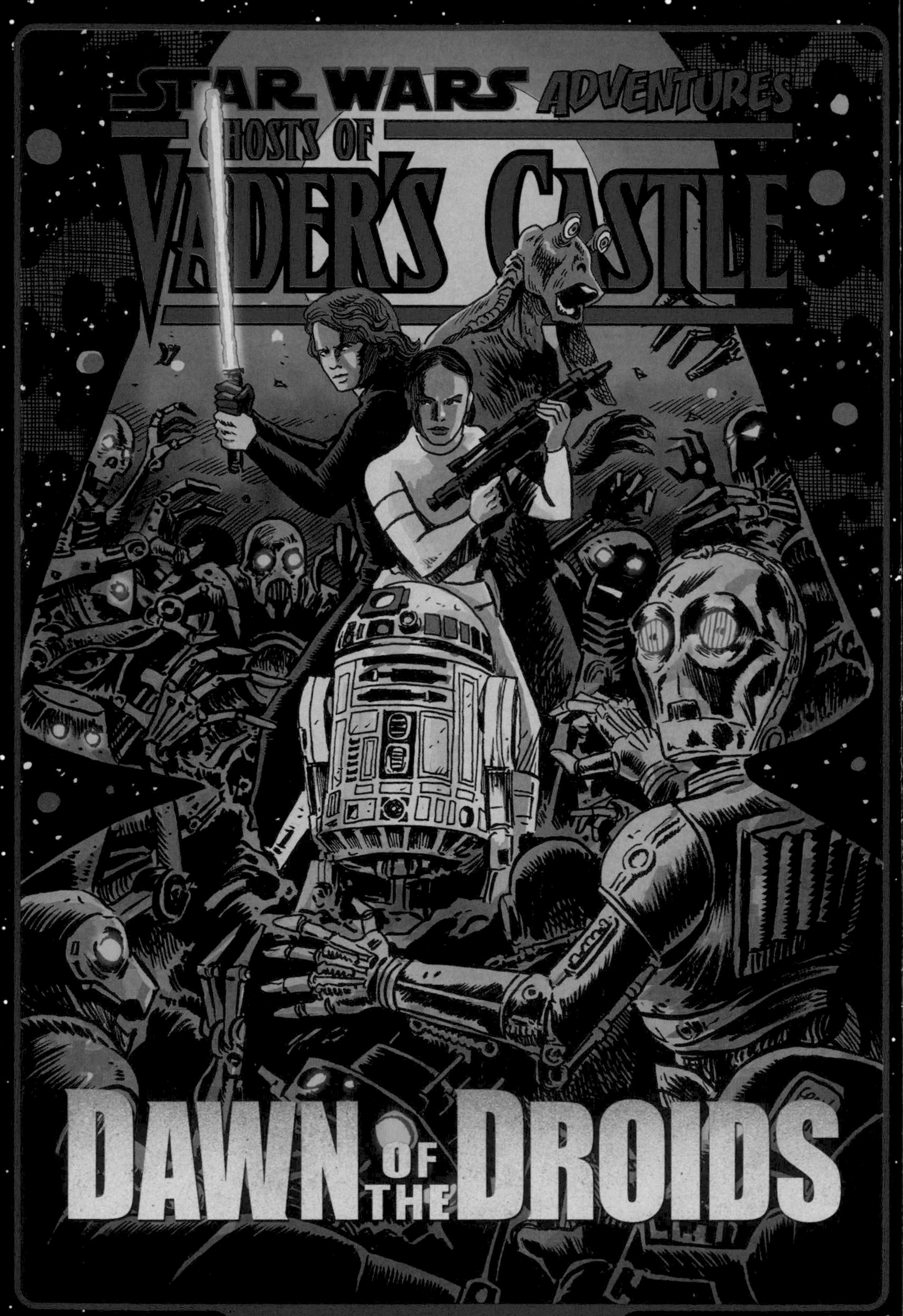
STAR WARS ADVENTURES
GHOSTS OF
VADER'S CASTLE
DAWN OF THE DROIDS
Art by Francesco Francavilla

FORTRESS VADER. MUSTAFAR.
THEY SAY YOU ARE *DEAD*, MASTER. THAT YOU WERE *DEFEATED*.
DEFEATED? THE SITH CAN *NEVER* BE DEFEATED.
I SHALL RISE AGAIN. MORE POWERFUL THAN EVER BEFORE. IT IS THE WILL OF THE *DARK SIDE*.

THE WILL. YESSS. TELL ME WHAT I MUST DO, MY LORD.
IS THE RITUAL PREPARED, VANEÉ? ARE YOU PREPARED?
YES, MASTER. ALL IS AS IT SHOULD BE.
THEN BEGIN...
AT LAST.
I CALL UPON THE IMMORTAL GODS OF THE SITH. ON MALEVOLENCE, ANGER, AND DREAD.
REACH ACROSS THE STARS, SPIRITS OF THE OBSIDIAN FLAME. SEEK OUT THOSE WHO HAVE WRONGED US.
FOR THE DARK LORD WILL RISE AGAIN.
THE DARK LORD WILL HAVE HIS REVENGE...

THE GRAF ARCHIVE. ORCHIS 2.
SO, ARE YOU COMING HOME ANY TIME SOON, LINA?
HOME? SINCE WHEN HAS ORCHIS BEEN HOME, MILO?
WELL, IT MAY NOT HAVE BEEN OUR HOME GROWING UP, BUT IT WAS HOME TO OUR FAMILY FOR CENTURIES.
I DIDN'T EVEN KNOW IT STILL EXISTED.
NONE OF US DID. NOT EVEN MOM AND DAD. AND TO THINK THAT THE EMPIRE WAS USING IT AS A LIBRARY ALL THOSE YEARS.
A SHAME THEY DIDN'T TREAT IT WITH MORE RESPECT WHEN THEY LEFT. YOU SHOULD SEE THE DAMAGE, MISTRESS LINA. THE DATABANKS THEY CORRUPTED. THE TEXTS THEY DESTROYED.
IF I HAD A HEART IT WOULD BE BROKEN.
HAS HE BEEN LIKE THAT ALL THE TIME?
CRATER? WHAT DO YOU THINK? HE'S HAPPIEST WHEN HE'S COMPLAINING.
I HEARD THAT.
GOOD!
BUT YOU WON'T BELIEVE THE THINGS THAT WERE LEFT BEHIND. RECORDS FROM THE NAMELESS PURGE. ART FROM THE OLD REPUBLIC.
EVEN WHAT APPEARS TO BE DIAGRAMS OF DARTH VADER'S CASTLE ON MUSTAFAR.

M-MUSTAFAR?
NO NEED TO LOOK LIKE THAT. I KNOW YOU DON'T LIKE TO TALK ABOUT WHAT YOU SAW WHEN YOU AND THE OTHERS CRASHED THERE*.
* SEE TALES FROM VADER'S CASTLE --HORRIFIED HEATHER
I JUST WISH I'D BEEN WITH YOU.
DON'T--WE BARELY GOT OUT ALIVE.
PROMISE ME YOU'RE NOT THINKING OF STAGING ONE OF YOUR EXPEDITIONS.
THOSE DAYS ARE LONG GONE, SIS.
I'M GLAD TO HEAR IT. LOOK, I'LL CALL BACK LATER. I HAVE A MEETING WITH GENERAL SYNDULLA.
HAVE FUN. SPEAK SOON.
LINA NEVER CHANGES, DOES SHE, CRATE? STILL TELLING ME WHAT TO DO.
YOUR SISTER IS ONLY WORRIED ABOUT YOU, MASTER MILO.
WELL, THERE'S NO NEED.
ALTHOUGH, I COULD DO WITH A CHANGE OF SCENE. I THINK ALL THIS STUFF IS GETTING TO ME.
I HAD THE STRANGEST DREAM THE OTHER DAY.
REMEMBER THAT REPORT WE FOUND FROM THE CLONE WARS? ABOUT THAT SENATOR AND HER JEDI BODYGUARD?
I DREAMT I WAS THE BODYGUARD. I MEAN, IT DIDN'T LOOK LIKE ME, BUT I WAS THERE, IN THE MIDDLE OF IT ALL...

IT DOESN'T MATTER IF THE SENATE THINKS RUBINERO IS IMPORTANT OR NOT, SEE-THREEPIO. THERE HAS BEEN A SETTLEMENT HERE SINCE THE EARLY DAYS OF THE HIGH REPUBLIC.
A SETTLEMENT WHICH HAS SUDDENLY STOPPED RESPONDING TO MESSAGES.

WELL, ISN'T THAT JUST TYPICAL.
LEAVE THE DROID ON THEIR OWN, WHY DON'T YOU?
KLUNK
AAAH!
IS SOMEONE THERE?
I DO HOPE YOU'RE FRIENDLY...
HRRRNNNNNN

I DON'T GET IT. WHERE ARE THE TOWNSFOLK?
WHYSA ONLY DROIDS? LOTSA LOTSA DROIDS.

BIG, HEAVY DROIDS! AAAH!

AND WHY DO YOU HAVE TO TOUCH EVERYTHING YOU SEE, JAR JAR?
MESA CURIOUS, DATS ALL.
KRASH

SPEAKING OF WHICH, HAS ANYONE SEEN THREEPIO? HE'S BEEN GONE A WHILE.
BWEEP-OO-WOOP

ARTOO'S SPOTTED HIM...

...BUT HE'S CERTAINLY LOOKED BETTER...
...HEY, THREEPIO. WHAT HAPPENED? WHERE'S YOUR ARM?
GRNNNNNNN.
WHAT THE--
--THREEPIO, WHAT ARE YOU DOING?

AND SINCE WHEN DID YOU GET SO *STRONG?*
AAAAAAH!
SSVVVVK
I'M SORRY ABOUT THAT, MY FRIEND, BUT...
...BUT...
...OKAY, THAT'S NOT GOOD.
REALLY NOT GOOD!
ARGH!
VZZZZZZ
SKLLLK

UH-OH! ANAKIN IS IN TROUBLE.
HE'S NOT THE ONLY ONE. SOMETHING IS *VERY WRONG* WITH THESE DROIDS.
RRRNNNNNNNNNNNNNNN
MESA COMEN ANI!
HNNF!
NO MESA NOT! OW!
THWAM

HELPEN MESAAAA!

JAR JAR!
GETTEM DEM OFF!
HUNNNNNNN...
I'M TRYING! BUT THESE THINGS REALLY AREN'T HELPING.
WHERE'S ANAKIN WHEN WE NEED HIM?
BECAUSE WE NEED HIM *NOW!*
KRASH

IF OBI-WAN WAS HERE, HE'D PROBABLY SAY I'M A LITTLE TIED UP...
...BUT HIS JOKES ARE AS OLD AS THE REPUBLIC ITSELF.
WHAT I DON'T GET IS WHY THIS IS HAPPENING IN THE FIRST PLACE?
IS IT THAT WEIRD ENERGY? A BATCH OF CORRUPTED OIL?
VVZZZZM
WHOSA CARES? WESA NEED TO GET OUTTA HERE. THEESA CLANKERS ARE NUTSEN!
THAT I CAN AGREE WITH.
FWWWWSH

BACK TO THE SHUTTLE!
ANAKIN--WHAT ARE YOU DOING? I THOUGHT YOU WANTED US TO RUN.
IT'S NOT ME! IT'S MY ARM!
I CAN'T CONTROL IT!
AAAH!
DON'T PANIC, ANI!
THWIP
MESA WON'T LET YOUSA DOWN!
SWIIIP

HHNG! THANKS--I GUESS.
NOW, GO!
SLEKK

NYAH! I THINK I PREFERRED THREEPIO WHEN HE WAS TERRIFIED OF EVERYTHING.
NUUUUUUU...

ARTOO!
WHEEP-WHEEEEP
THUNK
EEEEEEEEE
WHOOP--
--WHUUUUUU

OH, ARTOO.
RRRRUUUUUUU
NOT YOU TOO.

THERE'S NOTHING WE CAN DO FOR THEM, ANAKIN.
DON'T LET ARTOO'S *SACRIFICE* BE IN VAIN!
PZOW PZOW

FWOOOSH
MAAAASSSTURRRRR...

ANAKIN, ARE YOU...
I'LL LIVE, PADME, UNLIKE ARTOO AND THREEPIO. MAYBE THE SENATE WAS RIGHT TO STAY AWAY FROM RUBINERO.
WHAT I DON'T UNDERSTAND IS WHAT HAPPENED TO ALL THE SETTLERS?
"IT HAD TO BE THE DROIDS. THEY MUST HAVE GOT THEM ALL."
GUNK GUUUNK
"THEN WHERE WERE THE *BODIES?* WE WOULD'VE AT LEAST *SOME* REMAINS, SURELY?"

BEATS ME. WHAT DO YOU THINK, JAR JAR?

JAR JAR?
HNNNN...

HURRRRRR
JAR JAR-- NO. NOT YOU TOO!
AAARGH!
"--AND THAT'S WHEN I WOKE UP. FREAKY, EH?"

I KNOW I'LL NEVER LOOK AT DROIDS THE SAME WAY AGAIN.
NOT ***YOU***, OF COURSE, CRATE.
I KNOW YOU WOULD NEVER HURT ANYONE.
I GUESS IT WAS ONLY A DREAM.
AAAAA!
VZZAT
YES, ONLY A DREAM... I WOULD NEVER HURT ANYONE...

...UNLESS MY DARK LORD COMMANDS!
FRAN CAVIL LAF.21

STAR WARS ADVENTURES

GHOSTS OF VADER'S CASTLE

ATTACK OF THE 50 FOOT WOOKIEE

Art by Francesco Francavilla

THE GALACTIC SENATE. CHANDRILA.
CHANCELLOR MON MOTHMA-- PLEASE...
...ALL I NEED IS A SHIP.
A SHIP TO TAKE YOU TO MUSTAFAR, A PLANET IN AN AREA OF SPACE STILL UNDER IMPERIAL CONTROL.
I REALIZE THAT, BUT MY BROTHER HAS GONE MISSING. CRATER, TOO.
YOUR FAMILY'S DROID...
YES. THE LAST TIME I SPOKE TO THEM, MILO WAS TALKING ABOUT DARTH VADER'S CASTLE.
YOU THINK THAT'S WHERE HE'S GONE, CAPTAIN GRAF?
IN ALL HONESTY, SENATOR... I DON'T KNOW. NO ONE HAS HEARD FROM HIM FOR DAYS AND...
AND YOUR BROTHER HAS A HABIT OF MOUNTING EXPEDITIONS TO THE MOST INHOSPITABLE OF PLACES.
EXPEDITIONS FROM WHICH HE HAS ALWAYS RETURNED.
YES. BUT THIS TIME FEELS DIFFERENT.
I... I HAD A DREAM...

"...I DREAMT HE WAS TRAPPED IN VADER'S CASTLE... THAT HE COULDN'T ESCAPE... THAT IT WAS DEVOURING HIM...
"...IT WAS *AWFUL.*"

I'M SORRY, LINA... WHILE I RECOGNIZE THE DEBT WE OWE YOUR FAMILY, I SIMPLY CANNOT JUSTIFY SENDING A SHIP TO MUSTAFAR BECAUSE YOU HAD A BAD DREAM...
BUT IT'S MORE THAN THAT... I *KNOW* IT IS...

THE MATTER IS CLOSED. WE NEED TO CONCENTRATE ON REAL CONCERNS... LIKE THE THREAT THE EMPIRE STILL POSES.
YOUR BROTHER WILL RETURN SOON, OF THAT I'M SURE.

I WISH I COULD BE.

HERE, TAKE THIS...

SENATOR ORGANA?
IT'S THE NAME OF A BAR ON EMITA.
IF YOU'RE DETERMINED TO GO BACK TO MUSTAFAR-- AND I CAN SEE YOU ARE--YOU'LL NEED A PILOT CRAZY ENOUGH TO TAKE YOU...

"...AND THERE'S ONLY ONE SMUGGLER I KNOW WHO FITS THE BILL..."
HEY! WATCH WHO YOU'RE SHOVIN', BUDDY!

I SAID-- WATCH IT!
TWAK

CAN YOU BELIEVE THAT JOKER? INTERRUPTING A GUY WHEN HE'S TELLIN' A STORY...

...I DON'T KNOW WHAT THE GALAXY'S COMING TO...
THIS IS WHO LEIA THINKS I SHOULD HIRE?

JAXXON T. TUMPERAKKI.
CAPTAIN OF THE RABBIT'S FOOT.
NOW WHERE WAS I?
SMUGGLER. THIEF. SWINDLER.
THE GUY'S A LEGEND...
...FOR ALL THE WRONG REASONS.
OH, YEAH... IT'S THE STRANGEST THING. I'VE BEEN HAVIN' THE SAME DREAM NIGHT AFTER NIGHT.
WELL, MORE OF A NIGHTMARE REALLY.
A... NIGHTMARE?

"I'M ON KASHYYYK, HAVING A KNOCK-DOWN-DRAG-OUT FIGHT WITH THIS GRAY-HAIRED WOOKIEE IN WILD HEADGEAR...
"...AND JUST WHEN I THOUGHT THINGS CAN'T GET ANY WORSE...
"...GUESS WHO SHOWED HIS FACE..."
WELL, LOOK WHO IT IS.
SOLO?
HAVING TROUBLE, JAX?
YOU BET YOUR IMPROBABLY WELL-CONDITIONED HAIR I AM.
I'VE BEEN HIRED TO TRANSPORT A SHIP-LOAD OF SAAVA BERRIES TO GLUTTA THE HUTT AND THIS MOTH-EATEN ANTIQUE WON'T LET ME TAKE OFF.
I'M NOT SURPRISED, PAL. IT'S THE FESTIVAL OF BOUNTY.
BOUNTY? AS IN HUNTERS?
NO, AS IN THE HARVEST. NOTHING CAN BE TRANSPORTED FROM KASHYYYK DURING THE FESTIVITIES.
NO NUTS. NO FRUITS. NOT EVEN A SINGLE MUSHBLOOM. IT'S CONSIDERED BAD LUCK OR SOMETHING.
BAD LUCK? I'LL GIVE YA BAD LUCK. HOW LONG IS THIS FESTIVAL ANYWAY?
NOT THAT LONG. ONLY THREE MORE WEEKS.

THREE WEEKS? YOU'RE KIDDIN' ME. GLUTTA WILL MAKE LEPI STEW OF ME.
THAT'S IT. COME ON MEL, WE'RE OUTTA HERE.
WEP WEP
YOU'RE GONNA MISS ALL THE FUN.
FUN? SOLO WOULDN'T KNOW FUN IF IT HIT HIM IN THE DEFLECTOR SHIELD, BESIDES--
WHOOSH
--WE HAVE ALL THESE SAAVA BERRIES TO DELIVER.
"I THOUGHT I WAS GONNA TO HAVE THE LAST LAUGH, HAVING ALREADY SNUCK THE CONSIGNMENT ON BOARD THE RABBIT'S FOOT...
"...I COULDN'T HAVE BEEN MORE WRONG!"
HEY, CHEWIE. WHAT'S WRONG WITH EVERYONE?
RRRWAAA!
HRAAAA!
JAXXON TOOK THE BERRIES ANYWAY? OF COURSE HE DID. THAT GUY'S GONNA GIVE SCOUNDRELS A BAD NAME.
BUT THERE'S NO REAL HARM DONE, IS THERE? IT'S ONLY AN OLD SUPERSTITION, RIGHT?

MRAAAA!
CHEWIE?
"OF COURSE, I HAD NO IDEA WHAT WAS HAPPENING DOWN ON THE PLANET...
"...I WAS TOO BUSY CONGRATULATIN' MYSELF ON A SCAM WELL DONE."
GRAAAH!
I WONDER WHAT THESE THINGS TASTE LIKE ANYWAY?
UGH! LIKE LICKIN' A GAMORREAN'S ARMPIT, THAT'S WHAT! GIVE ME A JUICY BANTHA STEAK ANY DAY!
PTOO
HRAAAGAAA!
"TURNED OUT A BITTER TASTE IN MY MOUTH WAS THE LEAST OF MY WORRIES..."
NOW WHAT'S HAPPENING? WE CAUGHT IN A TRACTOR BEAM, MEL?
SPLAT

"IT WAS *NOT* A TRACTOR BEAM!"

IS THAT *CHEWBACCA?*
I THOUGHT WE WERE FRIENDS?
NOT ANYMORE!
KER-RUNCH
NO ONE CRUSHES THE *RABBIT'S FOOT,* RIGHT, MEL?
WAP-WAP-WAAAAAAA
BZAK
BZAK
NEED TO GET OUTTA HERE BEFORE I'M SQUASHED FLATTER THAN A SLIME-SLUG IN A TRASH COMPACTOR!
AW, MEL! NOT YOU, TOO!

HRAAAA
YEAH-- YOU CAN STOP ALL THAT BELLY-ACHING, YA BIG BULLY!
BOINK
WHY DON'T YA PICK ON SOMEONE YER OWN SIZE?
JAXXON! DON'T ANGER HIM!
YOU'RE ONLY MAKING THINGS WORSE!
WORSE? DID YOU SEE WHAT HE DID TO MY SHIP?
CRASH
HOLY HUTCH!
YEAH, I NOTICED!

THIS IS ALL YOUR FAULT.
HOW DO YOU FIGURE THAT?
MRAAA-GAA-HRRUUN
THE SPIRITS OF THE ANCESTORS HAVE TURNED CHEWBACCA INTO A VENGEANCE-FUELED MONSTER BECAUSE I STOLE A FEW MOLDY BERRIES?
THAT'S THE MOST RIDICULOUS THING I'VE EVER HEARD-- AND I'VE WATCHED ALL SEVENTEEN HOURS OF THE CALRISSIAN CHRONICLES!
BESIDES... IT LOOKS TO ME THAT HE'S WRECKIN' THE FOREST RATHER THAN PROTECTIN' IT!
KREECH
MRAAAA!
KRROOSH
AAARGH!
SEE WHAT I MEAN?

SOMEONE'S HAS TO STOP THAT MONSTER BEFORE HE WRECKS HALF OF KASHYYYK.
THAT'S NO MONSTER. THAT'S *CHEWIE!*
I'LL BE ABLE TO GET THROUGH TO HIM.
CHEWIE'S-- *NNG*--CHEWIE'S MY PAL...
...AND PALS ALWAYS LISTEN TO EACH OTHER.
AIN'T THAT RIGHT, BUDDY?
BUDDY?
DON'T LET ME DOWN, CHEWIE. NOT IN FRONT OF THE RABBIT.
GRRR

SWIPE
CHEWIE!
YEAH. YOU HANDLED THAT REAL GOOD, SOLO.
NOW WHAT'RE WE SUPPOSED TO DO?
HRUUUM
WHAT? THIS IS NO TIME TO BE THINKIN' OF FOOD, YOU LOONY!
BESIDES, I'VE ALREADY EATEN SOME OF YOUR SO-CALLED FRUIT AND IT'S ABSOLUTELY DISG--
--UFFMMF!
ACK!
WHY WOULD YA DO THAT, YOU LOUSY FLEABAG? OOOH, I FEEL...
...I FEEL REALLY WEEEEIRD!

RRAAWWRRH!
WHO'S THE GALAXY'S BIGGEST SMUGGLER NOW, FUZZ-FACE?
"TURNS OUT THAT CHEWIE WAS MORE THAN READY TO CUT ME DOWN TO SIZE--ME AND EVERYBODY ELSE FOR THAT MATTER!
WATCH WHERE YOU'RE WAVIN' THAT THING!
SKRASH

"AND SO WE WENT AT IT, ME AND THE OVERSIZED FUR-RUG, DESTROYIN' EVERYTHING IN OUR PATH. TREEHOUSES. BRIDGES. NOTHING WAS SAFE..."
"WHO WOULD'VE THOUGHT THAT OLD JAX COULD GO TOE-TO-TOE WITH THE MIGHTY CHEWBACCA? NOT ME, THAT'S FER SURE..."

"BUT IN THE END IT WAS JUST A CASE OF PUTTING MY BEST FOOT FORWARD!
KCHOP
"TURNS OUT THE OL' SAYING IS TRUE--THE BIGGER THEY ARE...
"...THE HARDER THEY FALL!"
HFFT!
KRASH
WILL YA LOOK AT THAT? THE MAGIC'S WEARIN' OFF.
SHAME. A GUY COULD GET USED TO LOOKIN' DOWN ON PEOPLE FOR A CHANGE.
AH, WELL. EASY COME, EASY GO.
YOU OKAY, CHEWIE OL' BUDDY? NO HARD FEELINGS, HUH?
NO HARD FEELINGS?!

DID YOU SEE WHERE WE LANDED? LOOK AT THE *FALCON*. IT'S IN PIECES. ***PIECES!***
UH-OH!
YEAH, YOU COULD SAY THAT, YOU NO-GOOD LEPI. HERE! GIMME ONE OF THOSE THINGS.
NOW, HAN. LET'S NOT DO ANYTHIN' HASTY.
MFFLE-SLFF
I'M ASSUMING THAT MEANS "THE LAST THING I WANT TO DO IS FALL OUT WITH MY OL' PAL JAX AND WE SHOULD ***DEFINITELY*** LET BYGONES BE BYGONES."
HHNNGG!
GULP
I'LL TAKE THAT AS A NO.

JAXXOOOON!
DOES NO ONE AROUND HERE KNOW HOW TO TAKE A JOKE?
WAAAH!
"CAN YOU BELIEVE IT? HAN SOLO *FINALLY* THE SIZE OF HIS EGO..."

...IS IT ANY WONDER I'VE NOT SLEPT A WINK SINCE.
YOU'RE NOT THE ONLY ONE.
WAA! WHAT ARE YOU DOIN' CREEPING UP ON A FELLA LIKE THAT?
YOU COULD'VE GIVEN ME A HEART ATTACK!
SENATOR ORGANA SENT ME.
PRINCESS LEIA? PRINCESS LEIA SENT YOU TO ME?
SURE. I NEED A PILOT.
THEN YOU'RE LOOKIN' IN THE WRONG PLACE, SWEETHEART.
MY DAYS OF DEALING WITH LEIA, SOLO, AND ALL THEIR SHENANIGANS ARE OVER.
AND I WOULDN'T ASK... NOT USUALLY... BUT I MEANT WHAT I SAID.
YOU'RE NOT THE ONLY ONE WHO'S BEEN HAVING NIGHTMARES. I'VE BEEN HAVING THEM AND THINK MY **BROTHER** WAS HAVING THEM BEFORE HE WENT MISSING.
THEY MEAN SOMETHING... I JUST KNOW IT... SOMETHING BAD...

WHO
OSHHHH
"--SOMETHING... EVIL."
WELCOME BACK TO MUSTAFAR, LOYAL DROID.
THANK YOU... MASTER. I HAVE BOUGHT THE SACRIFICE AS YOU COMMANDED.
YESSS...
SOON THEY WILL ARRIVE. ALL OF THEM.
AND LEARN THE TRUE MEANING OF FEAR.

Art by Francesco Francavilla

FORMER IMPERIAL OUTPOST. KARKEN, THE INNER RIM.
SIGH
REMEMBER WHEN LIFE WAS EXCITING, HUDD?
REMEMBER WHEN EVERY DAY MEANT DANGER AND ADVENTURE?
REMEMBER WHEN WE NEARLY DIED OVER AND OVER AGAIN?
REMEMBER WHEN I WAS TORTURED BY A MANIAC WITH AN ENERGY WEB?*
FTTZ
*SEE RETURN TO VADER'S CASTLE --HORRIFIED HEATHER.
WHAT WAS THAT?
NOTHING.
I'M JUST TIRED, THAT'S ALL. NOT BEEN SLEEPING PROPERLY. EITHER WAY, THIS IS AN IMPORTANT JOB. A USEFUL JOB.
YEAH, NOW SOUND LIKE YOU MEAN IT.
I DO, AS SOON AS WE REWIRE THIS OLD BASE--
FZZZT
THE NEW REPUBLIC CAN MOVE IN. I GET IT, HUDD--BUT DON'T YOU MISS THE OLD DAYS EVEN A LITTLE?

WHAT DO YOU THINK?
AAHHH!
AAH! NO ONE EVER SAID THIS PLACE HAD MYNOCKS!

GOTTA LOVE THOSE PEASLE REFLEXES.
CURL UP INTO A BALL AT THE FIRST SIGN OF TROUBLE.
WISH I COULD DO THE SAME.
REEEEEE
THUN

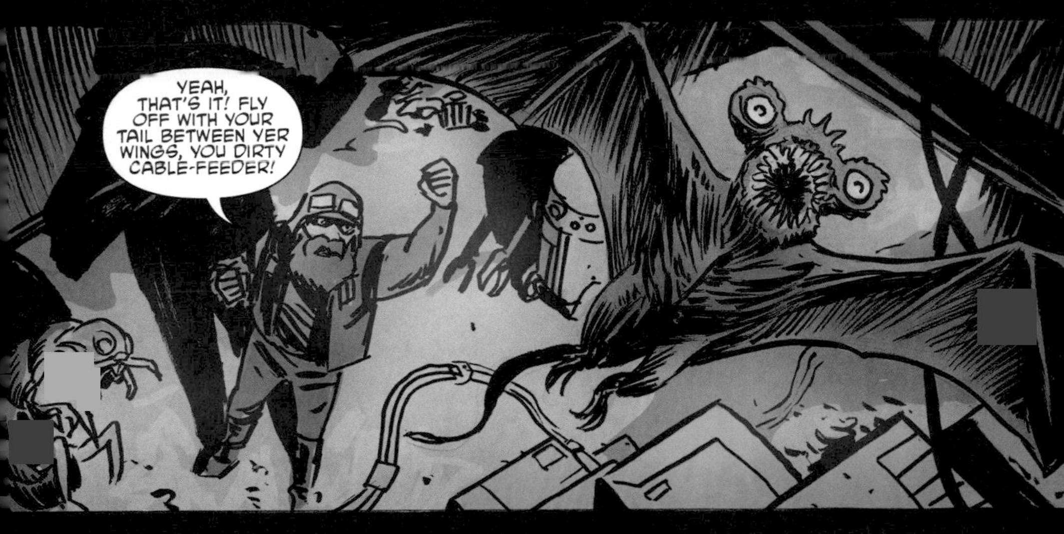
YEAH, THAT'S IT! FLY OFF WITH YOUR TAIL BETWEEN YER WINGS, YOU DIRTY CABLE-FEEDER!

WE'VE GOT TO FIND A NEW WAY TO DO THAT. MAYBE NEXT TIME I SHOULD THROW YOU?
DO YOU KNOW WHAT I'D LOVE TO SEE? A SMILE ON THAT BIG OLD FACE OF YOURS.
THAT I'D LOVE TO SEE.
WHAT'S REALLY GOING ON WITH YOU HUDD? WHAT'S THIS ALL ABOUT?

I TOLD YOU. I'VE NOT BEEN SLEEPING.
IT'S THESE DREAMS. THEY'RE DRIVING ME CRAZY... NIGHT AFTER NIGHT... ALWAYS THE SAME...

"I'M ON A SHUTTLE WITH LUKE SKYWALKER--
"--YEAH, YEAH, THERE'S NO NEED TO LOOK AT ME LIKE THAT... THE LUKE SKYWALKER...
"...I TOLD YOU IT WAS A DREAM...
"WE'RE ON A MISSION, LOOKING FOR OLD JEDI ARTIFACTS--AT LEAST, THAT'S WHAT HE TELLS ME WE'RE DOING..."
ARE YOU SURE I'M THE RIGHT MAN FOR THE MISSION, GENERAL... ER, I MEAN JEDI... I MEAN...
...WHAT DO I CALL YOU?
LUKE WILL DO JUST FINE.
AND YES... YOU'RE ABSOLUTELY THE RIGHT GUY FOR THE JOB.
CAPTAIN GRAF VOUCHED FOR YOU PERSONALLY.
SHE DID?
I-I MEAN, SHE DID... GREAT.
"BUT IT ISN'T GREAT. MY STOMACH IS CHURNING LIKE THE AKKADESE MAELSTROM.
"HOW COULD LINA OF ALL PEOPLE VOLUNTEER ME FOR SOMETHING LIKE THIS? ANCIENT ARTIFACTS?

"THE LAST TIME I'D LAID MY HANDS ON AN ANCIENT ARTIFACT I SPENT MONTHS IN THE CLUTCHES OF THAT SITH FANATIC VANEÉ ON MUSTAFAR...
"...NOT TO MENTION NEARLY BEING DECAPITATED BY DARTH VADER HIMSELF...
"...THE LAST THING I WANT TO DO WAS GO ON A TREASURE HUNT...
"...BUT I TELL MYSELF IT'S FINE. THIS IS LUKE SKYWALKER WE'RE TALKING ABOUT.
"HE'S PROBABLY TAKING ME TO SOME KIND OF GLEAMING JEDI TEMPLE ON A NICE SAFE PLANET, RIGHT?

"WRONG!"
T-THIS ISN'T RIGHT, SURELY? MAYBE WE TOOK A WRONG TURN SOMEWHERE AROUND C-CANOLISS.

THIS IS *EXACTLY* WHERE WE'RE SUPPOSED TO BE.
BWOOP-BEEEE
I KNOW, ARTOO. I MISS HIM, TOO.

"I HAVE NO IDEA WHO THEY'RE TALKING ABOUT. ALL I KNOW IS THAT I WANT TO FIND WHAT WE WERE LOOKING FOR AND GET OUT OF THE STINKIN' SWAMP.
"EVERYWHERE I LOOK I CAN FEEL EYES WATCHING ME FROM THE GLOOM...

"SHADOWS OF THE PAST..."
AAH! NO. IT CAN'T BE.
NOT HERE. NOT *HIM!*

HEY--WHAT'S WRONG?
SPLOSH

I-I THOUGHT...

...I THOUGHT I SAW SOMEONE I USED TO KNOW... BUT THERE'S NOTHING THERE.
S-SORRY.

I GET IT. DAGOBAH CAN BE DISORIENTATING, ESPECIALLY ON YOUR FIRST VISIT.
BUT IT'S OKAY. WE HAVEN'T GOT FAR TO GO. WHAT WE'RE LOOKING FOR IS JUST AROUND THIS--

--NO.
NO, THAT'S NOT POSSIBLE.
WHAT ISN'T?

WHAT'S HAPPENED?
"I DON'T KNOW WHY HE'S SO UPSET... IT'S JUST AN OLD HUT OUT IN THE MIDDLE OF NOWHERE...

"OR WHAT'S LEFT OF IT..."
BEWEEP
I KNOW, ARTOO. TOTALLY DEMOLISHED.
BUT WHO WOULD HAVE DONE THIS?

MAYBE THIS CAN TELL US.

SOME KIND OF HOLO-RECORDER.
COME TO DAGOBAH... THE REPUBLIC'S NEWEST DESTINATION.
CUTTING EDGE PLANET-SCAPING... LUXURY HOMES... EVERYTHING YOUR HEART DESIRES!
"YOU KNOW THE ADVERTS, RIGHT? PROPERTY DEVELOPERS MOVING INTO DUMPS THE GALAXY OVER... PROMISING THE STARS...

"THIS TIME THEY OBVIOUSLY GOT MORE THAN THEY BARGAINED FOR..."
RLO
YAAH! IT'S BACK!
THE MONSTER'S BACK!
WHAT'S THAT?!

AAH!
WATCH OUT! YOU'LL DAMAGE IT.
FTZZ

DAMAGE IT? IT NEARLY TOOK MY HAND OFF.
WHAT WAS THAT CREATURE?
I DON'T KNOW. I'VE NEVER SEEN ANYTHING LIKE IT... EVEN HERE.

WE JUST NEED TO KEEP AN EYE OUT FOR ANYTHING--

RLOOOON
UNUSUAL?
TERRIFYING?
BOTH?!

RAAAAAAR
WHAT IS IT?
CAREFUL, HUDD! DON'T GET IN THE WAY!
VSSSSM

SWLKK
AAARGH!
HUDD!

SPLOOSH

HUUUUDDD

SPLOOSH
HHH

LUKE?
ARTOO?

WHERE ARE YOU?
SSSSSSSSSSS

AAAH!
WHERE ARE YOU GOING, HUMAN?
YOU KNOW YOU'RE ALONE, DON'T YOU?

NO ONE'S COMING TO SAVE YOU THIS TIME. NOT LIKE BEFORE.
HH HH
"IT'S A LIE. I KNOW IT IS. ALL I NEED TO DO IS FIND LUKE SKYWALKER.
"HE'LL SAVE ME... IT'S WHAT JEDI DO...

"...AS LONG AS THERE'S BREATH IN THEIR BODIES..."
NO.
NO, NO, NO, NO...
AAH!
THUD

AT LEAST WE KNOW WHAT HAPPENED TO THE DEVELOPERS.
WHA--?

LISTEN TO ME, HUDD.
L-LISTEN TO YOU? HOW ARE YOU SPEAKING?
THE FORCE IS OUT OF BALANCE.

THAT CREATURE IS THE *SPIRIT OF THE SWAMP*.
RAAAR
IT WAS PROTECTING THE PLANET, FIRST AGAINST THE ZELTRONS, THEN AGAINST *US*.
YEAH? AND NOW IT'S BACK!
YOU MUST STOP IT, HUDD... FOR ALL OUR SAKES...
ME? HOW?
THE FORCE WILL PROVIDE... TRUST IN THE FORCE...
YOUR *LIGHTSABER?*
WHAT AM I SUPPOSED TO DO WITH THAT?

I'M NO JEDI!
"SOMEWHERE IN THE BACK OF MY MIND I KNOW IT'S A DREAM, EVEN AS I RUN FOR MY LIFE...

"BUT IT FEELS SO REAL..."
SNGG
AAH!

"TOO REAL.
"I CAN ALMOST HEAR LUKE'S VOICE IN MY HEAD. 'THE FORCE WILL PROVIDE, HUDD. YOU JUST NEED TO STOP RUNNING...'
GLUB
SPLOOSH

"YOU JUST NEED TO STAND YOUR GROUND!'"
GRAAA
OKAY THEN, YOU OVERGROWN SCUMSLUG... IF YOU WANT ME--

SVVMM
--THEN COME AND GET ME!

...

HA! I DON'T BELIEVE IT. I MUST BE SCARIER THAN I THOUGHT...

I NEVER DOUBTED YOU FOR A MOMENT.
LUKE? HOW?
I DON'T UNDERSTAND...
...PERHAPS I SHOULD TAKE THAT?

OH, OF COURSE... SORRY.
VZMM
I'VE TOLD YOU. THERE'S NO NEED TO APOLOGIZE...

...EVEN SPIRITS OF THE SWAMP KNOW NOT TO MESS WITH THOM HUDD!
"I DON'T REMEMBER MUCH AFTER THAT.. EVERYTHING IS SO MUDDLED...
"I MEAN... LUKE HAD TO BE RIGHT, YEAH? WHAT ELSE COULD'VE SCARED THE MONSTER AWAY?

"THERE WAS NO ONE ELSE THERE...

"NO ONE AT ALL..."
"AND THAT'S WHY YOU'RE SO JUMPY? BECAUSE OF A DREAM?"

BUT HAS TO MEAN SOMETHING, DOESN'T IT SKRITT?
SEEING VANEE AGAIN? EVEN IN A DREAM?
AND ALL THAT STUFF ABOUT TRUSTING THE FORCE?
WHAT IF IT WAS A WARNING FOR DANGERS TO COME?
SHAME NO ONE WARNED YOU ABOUT DISTURBING A MYNOCK'S NEST!
AARGH!
REEEEEEREEE
FLITTER FLIT FLIT
REEEREE
REE
REREEEEE
WHERE'S A LIGHTSABER WHEN YOU NEED ONE?
VROOOSH
LOOK LIKE THERE'S NO NEED.

WHAT A WRECK? WHO DO YOU THINK IT IS?
FOOOOSH
DON'T KNOW. DOESN'T LOOK LIKE A REPUBLIC CRUISER TO ME?
YEAH, THERE'S A REASON FOR THAT...
IT CAN'T BE--
--LINA?
WHAT ARE *YOU* DOING HERE?
LOOKING FOR YOU! MILO'S IN DANGER, HUDD! WE NEED TO GO BACK.
WE NEED TO GO TO **VADER'S CASTLE!**
FRAN CAVIL LAF. 21
HA HA HA HA HA

Art by Francesco Francavilla

THIS IS A BAD IDEA.
A *REALLY* BAD IDEA.
FOOM
HEY, DON'T LOOK AT ME, BEARDY!
I WASN'T THE JOKER WHO WANTED TO FLY TO *MUSTAFAR* OF ALL PLACES. I'M JUST THE RIDE OVER HERE.
THE RIDE WHO IS GOING TO GET US *KILLED!*

NAH, THAT'LL BE THE TIE FIGHTERS, LITTLE BUDDY.
OF COURSE, IF YOU HELPED INSTEAD OF MOANIN', WE'D BE THROUGH THIS BARRICADE IN NO TIME.
THOOM

THIS IS CRAZY! WE DON'T EVEN KNOW THAT MILO IS ON MUSTAFAR.
YOU HEARD WHAT LINA SAID, HUDD. ALL CLUES POINT TO VADER'S CASTLE.

AND THEN THERE ARE THOSE SPOOKY NIGHTMARES WE'VE ALL BEEN HAVIN'...
WE? I STILL DON'T REALLY KNOW WHO YOU ARE!

I'M JAXXON T. TUMPERAKKI, PAL. YOU DON'T LIKE IT, YOU CAN GET OFF MY SHIP.

A SHIP? IS THAT WHAT WE'RE CALLING THIS PIECE OF JUNK? IT'S A JOKE.
YOU WANNA SAY THAT AGAIN, BUG-BOY?
SKRITT! JAXXON! THAT'S ENOUGH!
EVERYONE NEEDS TO--

--STOP SHOUTING...?
HUDD? SKRITT?
WHERE DID YOU ALL GO?
COME TO THINK OF IT, WHERE ARE THE TIES?
THEY CAN'T HAVE JUST VANISHED.
YOU SURE ABOUT THAT?
THAT VOICE... THAT'S NOT JAXXON.
NO, LINA...

...IT'S NOT.
N-NEED TO FIND THE OTHERS. NONE OF THIS MAKES SENSE.
SENSE? WHAT ARE YOU TALKING ABOUT?
ONLY A CHILD THINKS THE GALAXY MAKES SENSE...
...BUT YOU ARE A CHILD AREN'T YOU, LINA?

WHO... WHO ARE YOU?
YOUR WORST NIGHTMARE.
AAH!
FWSH
YES. THAT'S IT. RUN, LITTLE GIRL.
I LIKE IT WHEN THEY RUN.
WHAT? NO!
LITTLE LINA GRAF, SO LOST. SO ALONE. JUST LIKE ALWAYS.
NO FAMILY. NO DROID. NOT EVEN YOUR BROTHER.

NO WAY TO ESCAPE...
SHHM
THIS ISN'T REAL. NONE OF IT. I'M NOT A KID ANYMORE. I'M NOT, I'M--
AAH!
TRPP
NO... CRATER.
CRATER, IS THAT YOU?
SHH, MISTRESS LINA...
...HE'LL HEAR YOU...
LIIIINAAAA...

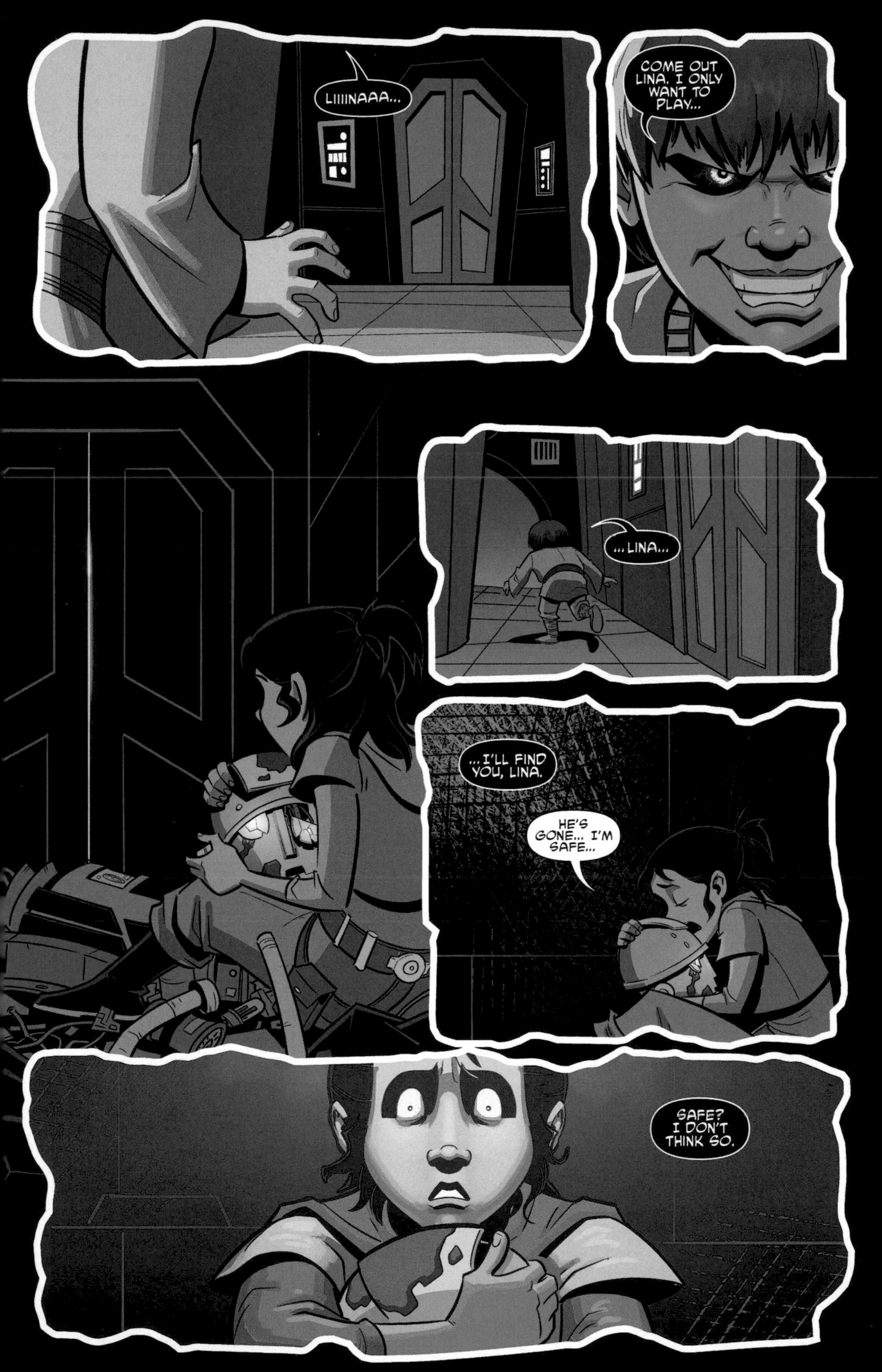
LIIINAAA...
COME OUT LINA. I ONLY WANT TO PLAY...
...LINA...
...I'LL FIND YOU, LINA.
HE'S GONE... I'M SAFE...
SAFE? I DON'T THINK SO.

FOOSH
THIS IS WHERE THE FUN BEGINS.
AAAH!

AAH!
SHOOSH
I TOLD YOU...YOU CAN'T ESCAPE. THERE'S NO POINT IN TRYING.
FWOOSH
Y-YOU DON'T SCARE ME--
--WHOEVER YOU ARE.

RUN, MISTRESS LINA.
WHAT ABOUT YOU?
I'M ALREADY FINISHED. SAVE YOURSELF.
"SAVE MASTER MILO."
"SAVE YOURSELF. SAVE MILO."
HOW BRAVE. HOW NOBLE. I ONLY HAVE ONE QUESTION, DROID--
--WHO'S GOING TO SAVE YOU?
AAAAAH!

DID YOU HEAR THAT, LINA?
FSSSSSN
HE'S GONE, LINA. THEY'RE ALL GONE.
YOUR RIEND YOUR PARENT
YOUR ITTLE BROTHE
NO.
IT'S LIES. NONE OF IT'S TRUE. IT'S--

--OOF!

MILO?

OH, MILO. I FOUND YOU. YOU'RE SAFE. YOU'RE SAFE NOW.

NO, LINA.
NYAH--
--YOU JUST DON'T GET IT.
MILO?

ARGH!
THERE'S NO HOPE FOR ME NOW.
MILO! WHAT'S WRONG?!
WHAT'S HAPPENING TO YOU?
"YOU NEED TO FORGET ABOUT ME, LINA.
"DO WHAT CRATER SAID... SAVE *YOURSELF!*"
I CAN'T DO THAT, MILO. I *WON'T*.
I'LL STOP WHATEVER THIS IS. I'LL STOP *VADER*.
THAT'S JUST IT...
...SISTER...

...I AM VADER.
VADER REBORN.
VADER RENEWED.
HK
VADER TRIUMPHANT!

GASP
WHAT... WHERE?
HEY, SLEEPY HEAD. YOU AWAKE BACK THERE?
JAXXON? IS THAT YOU?
WHO ELSE WOULD IT BE? HOPE YOU CAUGHT A LITTLE SHUT EYE. WE'RE APPROACHING MUSTAFAR.
IT WAS A NIGHTMARE. JUST ANOTHER NIGHTMARE.
YOU THERE?
YEAH, JAX. I'M HERE. I JUST...
...I'LL BE WITH YOU IN FIVE, OKAY?
ROGER THAT. WE'LL--
--AARGH!
JAX? WHAT'S HAPPENED?
JAXXON!

WHAT DID I TELL YOU, GIRL?
YOUR FRIENDS ARE GONE, AS IS ANY HOPE YOU HAVE OF SAVING YOUR BROTHER.

IT'S OVER--
--AND SO ARE YOU.
VSSSK
AAA--

--AAH!
LINA?
HUDD? I...
YOU FELL ASLEEP THERE FOR A MOMENT.
THE DREAMS... THEY'RE GETTING WORSE...
YOU'RE TELLING ME, LADY.
HECK OF A TIME TO TAKE A NAP, THOUGH. WE'VE ARRIVED.
ON MUSTAFAR?
THAT'S WHERE YOU WANTED TO GO, AIN'T IT?
FWOOOSH

CAN'T SAY I LIKE WHAT THEY'VE DONE TO THE PLACE.
THIS IS IT? DOESN'T LOOK *THAT* SCARY.
DOESN'T LOOK... THIS WAS THE HOME OF *DARTH VADER,* JAXXON. DID YOU EVER MEET DARTH VADER?
WELL, ACTUALLY...
BECAUSE *WE* DID--AND WE BARELY ESCAPED.
LINA, WE NEED TO KEEP OUR HEADS. IF MILO *IS* IN THERE...

I KNOW, HUDD. I KNOW. AND I'M SORRY. YOU OF ALL PEOPLE MUST BE--
SCARED OUT MY WITS? WISHING I'D NEVER EVEN HEARD THE *WORD* MUSTAFAR?
IT'S THE DREAMS, LINA. THEY'RE GETTING TO US ALL.

AND DREAMS AREN'T REAL...

YOU'RE RIGHT, HUDD. THAT'S ALL THEY ARE... DREAMS.

"DREAMS CAN'T HURT YOU."

Art by Francesco Francavilla

FORTRESS VADER. MUSTAFAR.
HURRY, HUDD.
I AM HURRYING, LINA.
I COULD ALWAYS KICK IT DOWN FOR YA?
I DON'T NEED YOU TO KICK IT DOWN, JAXXON.
LOCKS LIKE THIS JUST TAKE TIME TO OVERRIDE AND--
LINA? LINA, ARE YOU THERE?
MILO?
MILO, WE'RE HERE... ON MUSTAFAR. WHERE ARE YOU?
HE'S HURTING ME, LINA. I NEED YOU. PLEASE, HELP ME!
WE'RE TRYING. I PROMISE YOU, WE'RE TRYING!
THAT DOES IT! STAND ASIDE, BEARDY!
HEY!
HE'S DIRECT, I'LL GIVE HIM THAT.
KCHOP
NO ONE APPRECIATES CRAFTMANSHIP ANYMORE.
WE'RE IN. THAT'S ALL THAT MATTERS.
YEAH. BUT WHO ELSE IS IN HERE WITH US, SKRITT? THAT'S WHAT I'M WORRIED ABOUT.
WHO DO YOU EXPECT TO FIND, BIG GUY?
VADER'S DEAD AND GONE. HE'S TOAST.
YEAH?

VZZZZM
YOU WANNA TELL HIM THAT?
HOLY HUTCH! CAN'T ANYONE STAY DEAD IN THIS GALAXY? NEXT YOU'LL TELL ME THAT OL' PRUNE-FACE IS OUT THERE SOMEWHERE!
ZOW ZOW
PLEASE DON'T TEMPT FATE, JAXXON.
SVVVK
BLASTERS ARE NO GOOD. THERE'S ONLY ONE THING FOR IT.
SURELY YOU DON'T...
YOU GOT ANY BETTER IDEAS?

HNNG!
THIS IS NEVER GONNA WORK!
FWOOSH
KRAK

IT WORKED!
YES--AND IT WAS TOO EASY!
THUD
THUD
THUD
LIEUTENANT HUDD? MISTRESS LINA?
IS THAT YOU?
HUH! HE USED TO SOUND SCARIER!
YOU THINK?
CRATER!
OH, MISTRESS LINA. I'M SO SORRY. THERE WAS A SIGNAL... IT SCRAMBLED MY PROCESSORS... MADE ME DO THE MOST TERRIBLE THINGS...
...I-I BROUGHT MASTER MILO TO HIM...

WHO? WHO DID THIS TO YOU, CRATER?
THAT ABOMINABLE MAN... DARTH VADER'S SNAKE OF A SERVANT...
VANEÉ?

VANEÉ IS STILL ALIVE?
I KNEW IT.

WHAT DID I TELL YOU, SKRITT? THE DREAMS... THE DREAMS WERE A WARNING.
YOU CAN DO THIS, HUDD. WE ALL CAN. BECAUSE WE'RE HERE TOGETHER. DO YOU HEAR ME?
CRATER--CAN YOU SHOW US WHERE MILO IS?
HEY--YOU SURE WE CAN TRUST HIM, LADY? HE WAS WORKING FOR THE OTHER SIDE.
I TRUST CRATER WITH MY LIFE, JAX.
HMM. IF I HAD A CREDIT FOR EVERY TIME SOMEONE I TRUSTED SHOT ME IN THE BACK...
I'D NEVER DO SUCH A THING... NOT NOW THAT I'M IN MY RIGHT MIND. TECHNICIAN SKRITT CORRECTED MY CIRCUITS.
OF COURSE I CAN TAKE YOU TO MASTER MILO--

--I JUST HOPE YOU CAN HELP *HIM*.
WE NEED TO GET HIM OUT OF THERE.
JUST WAIT A THRUSTER-BURNIN' MINUTE.
IF YER BROTHER'S FLOATIN' IN BACTA, THEN WHO WAS CHATTIN' ON THE COMM? DOES *NO ONE* ELSE THINK THAT'S A LITTLE SCREWY?
WE CAN WORRY ABOUT THAT LATER, JAXXON. ONCE MILO'S--
DEET DEET DEET
AAAAAA!

FRAN CAVIL LAF. 21

MISTRESS LINA?
MISTRESS LINA? OH, PLEASE WAKE UP.

IT'S A LITTLE TOO LATE FOR THAT, MY MECHANICAL FRIEND.
OH, NO... NO, NO, NO, NO, NO.
YOU STAY AWAY FROM HER, DO YOU HEAR? HAVEN'T YOU DONE ENOUGH?

ENOUGH?

"I'VE ONLY JUST STARTED..."

I'M SORRY, SIS. THIS IS ALL MY FAULT.
NO, IT'S NOT. IT WAS VANEÉ. HE WAS BEHIND IT ALL. CONTROLLING CRATER. USING YOU AS BAIT.

HE-HE-HE-HE
DO YOU HEAR THEM, MASTER? THEY THINK I ONLY CONTROLLED THE DROID.
DON'T THEY REALIZE THEY WERE ALL MY PUPPETS... THAT I USED THEIR OWN DREAMS AGAINST THEM, DRAWING THEM BACK TO THE CASTLE.

THE NIGHTMARES... THEY WERE YOU?
NO ONE IS SAFE FROM THE SITH, NOT EVEN WHEN THEY SLEEP.
I KNEW YOU WOULD COME. LOVED ONES IN DANGER? NEW MONSTERS TO FIGHT? HOW COULD YOU RESIST?

THIS IS ALL VERY INTERESTIN', BUT THERE IS ONE THING THAT DOESN'T MAKE SENSE.
I GET YOU HAVE A HISTORY WITH THESE SAD SACKS, BUT WHY GIVE ME NIGHTMARES? WHAT HAVE I GOTTA DO WITH ANY OF THIS?

ACTUALLY, I WAS WONDERING THE SAME THING.
WHO ARE YOU AGAIN?

WELL, AIN'T THAT JUST CHARMIN'!
MAYBE YOU ATE A BAD CARROT BEFORE HITTING THE SACK...
SHUT YER FACE.

YOU ALL MUST BE SILENT. THERE IS MUCH TO DO.
THE HOUR APPROACHES.
THE HOUR? HOUR FOR WHAT?
THE VILLAIN AIMS TO REVIVE HIS MASTER, MISTRESS LINA.
HIS MASTER? AS IN DARTH VADER?!
I HATE TO BREAK IT TO YOU, VANEE, BUT VADER IS GONE. I WAS ON ENDOR... I SAW THE DEATH STAR EXPLODE. YOUR MASTER'S DEAD.
AS YOU WERE THERE WHERE HE PERISHED, SO YOU SHALL BE HERE WHEN HE RISES AGAIN. NO... MORE THAN THAT...
...YOU SHALL BE THE MEANS OF HIS RESURRECTION.
I DON'T THINK SO.
GASP
YES, MASTER. I HEAR YOU, MASTER.
HE'S NUTTIER THAN A GRUFFLE-CAKE, THIS ONE.
THE MOMENT HAS COME.
I RELEASE THE VAPORS JUST LIKE YOU TAUGHT ME. LET THEM GUIDE YOUR PATH.
KLUNK

KOFF KOFF
WHAT IS THIS STUFF?
FUMES FROM THE LAVA PITS BENEATH THE CASTLE. IT'S ALL-- HACK --ALL PART OF HIS SITH MAGIC.
THIS ISN'T MAGIC, MILO--
COFF COFF
--IT'S MADNESS!
DO YOU HEAR HER, MASTER? SHE DOUBTS YOU. DOUBTS YOUR POWER.
SOON SHE WILL BELIEVE. SHE WILL KNOW.
ALL WILL BECOME CLEAR WHEN SHE IS ELEVATED. WHEN SHE BECOMES THE VESSEL FOR YOUR SPIRIT.
WHEN I BECOME THE WHAT NOW?!
SPEAK, OH LORD. SPEAK AND WE SHALL LISTEN.
RISE FROM THE ASHES, AS IT HAS BEEN FORETOLD. SPREAD YOUR DARK ARMS ACROSS THE GALAXY. VADER REBORN!
VADER IMMORTAL!

YES... I AM HERE, MY SERVANT. I *LIIIVE*--
ER... EVERYONE CAN HEAR THAT, RIGHT?
PLEASE TELL ME YOU CAN HEAR THAT.

--AS DO THEIR *NIGHTMARES*.
AAARGH! THE THING FROM MY DREAM! IT'S HERE! REALLY HERE!

NO, HUDD. NO, IT *ISN'T*. IT'S JUST THE FUMES. THEY'RE MAKING US SEE THINGS THAT AREN'T THERE.
LIES!
MAKING US *HEAR* THINGS TOO, JUST LIKE VANEÉ. LINA'S RIGHT.
ALL THOSE YEARS IN THE DARK... HE'S BEEN DRIVEN *MAD*.

YUP. THAT'S GOTTA BE IT.
WHAT DID YOU SAY, BOSS? IT'S JUST A DREAM. AND DREAMS CAN'T HURT US.

FOOL!
AAGH!
DO NOT UNDERESTIMATE THE *POWER* OF THE DARK SIDE.

YES... YES! AND NOW THE SCREAMING STARTS! THE GHOSTS ARE HERE! THE AGE OF THE SITH IS UPON US! A NEW EMPIRE OF DARKNESS. HIS EMPIRE.
IT WON'T WORK, VANEÉ. VADER'S NEVER COMING BACK. HE'S--

NO.

NO, IT'S NOT POSSIBLE.
FINALLY, AFTER ALL THE INDIGNITIES, ALL THE TRICKS. FINALLY, SHE UNDERSTANDS...
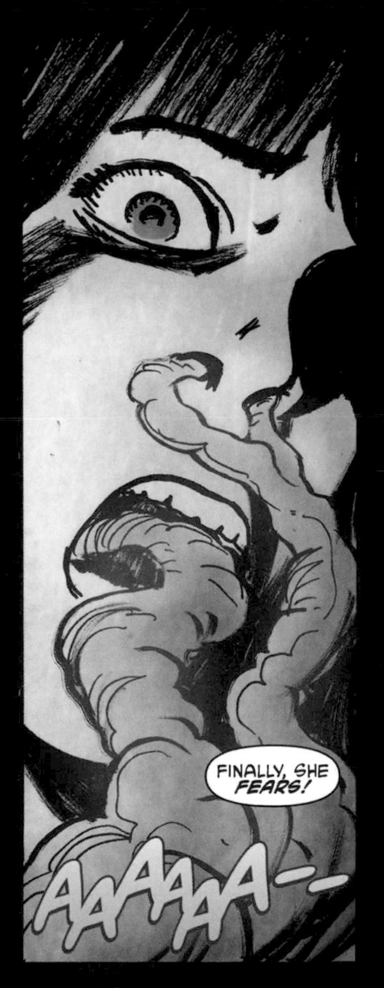
FINALLY, SHE FEARS!
AAAAAA--

M-MASTER?
MASTER, IS THAT YOU?

VA... NEE...

RELEASE ME THIS INSTANT.
NO ONE BINDS DARTH VADER. *NO ONE!*

A-AT ONCE, MY LORD.
Y-YOU HAVE RETURNED TO ME.
DEET CLIKK

IT WAS THE WILL OF THE *FORCE*.
AND W-WHAT DOES THE FORCE WILL NOW, OH DARK ONE? WHAT TERROR SHALL WE UNLEASH UPON THE GALAXY?

FIRST THINGS FIRST. WE MUST DEAL WITH THE PRISONERS.
VSSSKK

LINA. LINA, DON'T DO THIS.
IT'S *ME*. IT'S YOUR *BROTHER*.

YES. I KNOW *EXACTLY* WHO YOU ARE--

--WHICH IS WHY I'M GETTING YOU OUT OF HERE!
VZZZZK
WHAT? NO! THIS ISN'T POSSIBLE. THE SPIRIT OF MY LORD CONSUMED YOU. I SAW IT WITH MY OWN EYES.
THAT'S THE TROUBLE WITH THESE FUMES. THEY MAKE YOU SEE WHAT YOU MOST FEAR--AND IN YOUR CASE THAT'S DEFINITELY YOUR MASTER.
THAT WAS BEFORE HE MET ME! THIS IS FOR CRATER!
THAK
OOF!
THUDD
NO!
CLANK

ONE H-HECK OF A PUNCH MILO, BUT HOW DO WE GET OUT OF HERE?
I CAN'T SEE ANYTHING IN ALL THIS SMOG.
THERE! THAT MUST BE LINA!
VZZZM
FOLLOW THE LIGHT!
NO, YOU CAN'T LEAVE ME HERE. YOU CAN'T LEAVE ME TRAPPED!
WHY VANEE?
ISN'T THIS WHAT YOU WANTED? ISN'T THIS WHAT YOU HOPE FOR?
NOOO...
THIS IS THE WAY IT SHOULD BE... MASTER AND SERVANT... TOGETHER...

...TOGETHER FOR AL ETERNIT
AAAAIEEEEEEE
TRAPPED IN A LIVING NIGHTMARE. I ALMOST FEEL SORRY FOR THE GUY.
ALMOST.
KEEP MOVING, HUDD. WE'RE NEARLY THERE.
I'VE NEVER BEEN SO GLAD TO SEE MY SHIP.
WAIT! WHERE'S LINA?

RIGHT HERE, LITTLE BROTHER.
LINA. I KNEW YOU WOULD COME FOR ME.
ALWAYS, MILO. ALWAYS.
ALTHOUGH, I COULD'VE DONE WITHOUT THIS SABER RUNNING OUT OF JUICE THE MOMENT VANEÉ WAS TRAPPED.

BUT... IF IT WASN'T YOU... WHOSE LIGHTSABER DID WE FOLLOW?
MAYBE IT WAS A *GHOST!*
WOOOO!
STOP TEASING HIM, JAX.

YOU DON'T THINK THE RABBIT'S RIGHT, DO YOU LINA?
WHOOSH

RELAX, HUDD. IF THERE'S ONE THING THIS *NIGHTMARE* HAS TAUGHT ME--

"--THERE'S NO SUCH THING AS GHOSTS."
HEH.
FRAN CAVIL
THE END

Art by Derek Charm

Art by Derek Charm

Art by Derek Charm

Art by Derek Charm

Art by Derek Charm

Art by Megan Levens • Colors by Charlie Kirchoff

Art by Megan Huang